A College Mystery

by

A.P. Baker

A facsimile re-publication

Ostara Publishing

First Published by W Heffer Publishers 1918

Ostara Publishing Edition 2016

ISBN 9781909619401

A CIP reference is available from the British Library

Every reasonable effort has been made by the Publisher to establish whether any person or institution holds the copyright for this work. The Publisher invites any persons or institutions that believe themselves to be in possession of any such copyright to contact them at the address below.

Printed and Bound in the United Kingdom
Ostara Publishing
13 King Coel Road
Colchester
CO3 9AG
www.ostarapublishing.co.uk

Arthur Ponsford Baker was born in 1873 at Algoa Bay in the Cape Colony. He was educated at some stage in both Cheltenham and Bristol and in 1892 he went up to Cambridge. Eventually he became a lecturer in history at Christ's College. He died either late 1918 or in early 1919.

Thanks and Acknowledgments

Thanks go to Richard Reynolds for inspiring this re-issue.

The cover pictures are
reproductions of the original dust jacket and its spine.

Thanks are made to Christs College Library for providing the article, by Michael Wyatt, published in the 1998 edition of *Christ's College Magazine*.

A College Mystery – a Further Mystery?

Michael Wyatt

There is one very curious story about Christ's College which I am very certain has never been told although it was often referred to in my family. A.P. Baker wrote a short book – some 76 pages – about Christ's College that was published in 1918 just a few months before the author's death. It was called *A College Mystery*.

A lifelong friend of my father's came to Cambridge for a social visit. The date is not certain, but this is not material to the story. If a date had to be given then it was probably between 1928 and 1932. My father put my uncle Sam up in his rooms in college. Capt. Sam Wheeler R.N. (Eng.) was my father's third cousin and had fought at the Battle of Jutland, probably below decks. He had been a naval officer since the early years of the century. I mention this because I want to emphasise that my uncle had had a tough background and it was inconceivable that he was given to hearing things that go bump in the night.

My father's rooms were in the Fellows' Building. They were the rooms which way back in the 19th Century had been occupied by Mr. Round, if we are to follow the story in *A College Mystery*. My father was a Fellow of Christ's. The rooms were on 'A' staircase first floor and which, when viewing the building from Second Court, were on the right of the staircase. They were at one time occupied by Arthur Shipley before be became Master. This was a little before my father's time. (It is not inconceivable they were occupied by my father when Shipley moved out to The Lodge on his election as Master.) The date Sam Wheeler stayed was May 29th. This was the date my father's rooms were reputed to be haunted according to the story. I know that my parents gave no thought to the matter beforehand and nobody told my uncle about the story.

According to my mother, the events of that night in the Fellows' Buildings were traumatic. In the morning Sam Wheeler was white from his night's experience. He had not slept at all. When I asked my mother to tell me more of what had happened she told me that Sam had heard throughout the night foot-steps on the stairs and other noises such as knockings and bumps. Of course it could be argued that these noises had been taken straight from the book which my mother had read. Be that as it may the effect on my uncle, the old sea dog, was considerable. There were no doubts about the truth of my mother's account. I knew my uncle well in later years but I cannot be specific about any future references he made to that night: they were casual and dismissive as though he thought in retrospect he had made a fool of himself. He was possibly upset that an account of these events had reached me, who was a generation junior to him.

There is only one explanation that comes within my own experience. Was there a heatwave at the time? Later my father had his rooms on First Court backing onto Christ's Lane. I myself spent some nights in those rooms one Long Vacation. There was a heatwave. The daytime temperatures were in the nineties. The evenings were very warm but cooled as the, night proceeded. I listened to the cacophony of sounds produced by the old timbers. I found it eerie, even though I had previous experience of living in my undergraduate rooms in First Court exactly opposite my father's rooms in hot weather although not to the degree experienced in my father's rooms. Were these the noises my uncle had heard? But, of course, the First Court was built in early Tudor times whilst the Fellows' Building appears to have been built just as the Civil War was breaking out. Not likely to be so susceptible to such heatwave noises.

Michael Wyatt BA 1950 MA 1974 wrote *Memories about a father: the late Travers Wyatt OBE (mil).*

Ostara Cambridge Crime Titles

All titles available from
Heffers
20 Trinity Street Cambridge CB2 3NG
Telephone 01223 463222
Email literature@heffers.co.uk

THE FELLOWS' BUILDING, CHRIST'S COLLEGE, CAMBRIDGE.

Reading from left to right, first floor, Round's rooms are windows 2 and 3, and Collier's 8 and 9. The central arch is the entrance to the garden.

A COLLEGE MYSTERY

PREFACE

My thanks are due to the Master and Fellows of Christ's College for permission to make the drawings of the College and to use the College arms; to the Provost of Eton for reading through the manuscript of this little book and for kindly comment; and to Major J. V. Bibby, D.S.O., and to Captain P. G. Marr, R.A.F., for help in arranging for the illustrations. Especially I have to thank Mr. F. H. Round for the drawings themselves and for his interest in making them.

To the friends to whom the story was first read in my rooms in February I need not here express my thanks for their kindness, especially to those to whose constant encouragement I owe so much.

Christ's College, Cambridge.
October, 1918.

CONTENTS

LIST OF ILLUSTRATIONS

EDITOR'S PREFACE

I WAS first interested in the apparition in the Fellows' Garden through communications from friends who had kept in the Fellows' Building and, therefore, had rooms overlooking the Garden. The similarity of their accounts was striking, and some of them were made without knowledge that others had made them too.

It was not till years later that the papers of Simon Goodridge came into my possession. I was much interested to find amongst them documents which appear to bear upon the history of the apparition, which my friends alleged that they had seen. I have, therefore, arranged the papers in order, putting my friends' communications first and the Goodridge papers second.

The Goodridge papers consist of (1) The Record of Christopher Round, (2) Newspaper extracts collected by Goodridge, (3) Goodridge's own recollections.

I have added nothing to the papers as left by Goodridge, except a few explanatory footnotes. I have divided Round's Record into sections, for the sake of clearness.

I should state also that among Goodridge's papers I found a short note to the effect that Round's Record was not to be published until at least fifty years after his death. The note was in the same handwriting as the Record, and is, presumably, Round's own. The note explains why Goodridge never made the Record known.

Goodridge left a postscript to his collection of papers in which he says that, as far as he could judge, *most* of the statements made by Round in his Record are true. The word *most* is underlined.

More than the fifty stipulated years have gone by, and I am giving the papers publicity, believing that the recalling of a forgotten mystery and tragedy will be of interest, especially to those who know Cambridge and are familiar with the scenes amid which the events took place.

A. P. B.

Christ's College, Cambridge.
1918.

A COLLEGE MYSTERY

The story of the apparition in the Fellows' Garden at Christ's College,
Cambridge

I

COMMUNICATIONS FROM PAST RESIDENTS IN THE FELLOWS' BUILDING

THE most relevant of the communications that have been made to me concerning the apparition in the Fellows' Garden have come from G. E. B., who was at Christ's ten years or so before my time; from F. S. S., of my own year; and from G. K. N. and F. T. Y., who were here not more than ten years ago. They all stipulated that their actual names should not be inserted. They all kept in the Fellows' Building. G. E. B. had the rooms on Staircase A on the second floor, to the left of the stairs when facing the Garden. He was therefore one floor above the room once occupied by Round, and not immediately over it. The windows of his rooms command a fine view of the Garden.[1] F. S. S. had the rooms in the similar position on Staircase B, and therefore in the same position relatively to Collier's old rooms as G. E. B.'s were to Round's.[2] He also had a good view of the Garden. G. K. N. and F. T. Y. occupied the two sets of attics at the top of Staircase A, and were there for three years together. They could not see the Garden from these rooms, but they often spent part of the evening on the leads looking over the parapet.

---

[1] These rooms were for some years occupied by the Rev. J. W. Cartmell, for many years Senior Tutor of Christ's. They will thus be recollected by most Christ's men. They are now occupied by Mr. J. T. Saunders, Junior Fellow of Christ's.

[2] These rooms are those now occupied by Mr. S. G. Campbell, Bursar of Christ's.

All these have assured me that on many occasions, generally on clear summer nights, when there was bright moonlight, they have observed the figure of a man emerge on the lawn from under the great chestnuts, on the left, and walk slowly and deliberately, with bent head, as far as the great yew and the weeping ash. There he invariably stopped suddenly and turned towards the may tree, and then faced up the garden again, on the right, and either disappeared by the green beech, or came out on the lawn past the great copper beech, skirted the border of that bed, and then faded from view by the old elm[3] near where the sun-dial now stands. They described the figure as that of a tall, heavy, elderly man, dressed in black, with a swallow-tailed coat and high collar and stock. He sometimes raised his face; but the sudden halt at the great yew was invariable.

There were some discrepancies in these accounts. G. E. B. says that he remembers seeing him carrying what looked like a heavy crooked stick, but all the others maintain that his hands were folded behind his back. F. S. S. says that he has seen him wearing a cap and gown, and, as far as he remembered, he usually did so. The others all agree that he had no gown, or overcoat, and wore a broad brimmed black beaver hat. He was, as I said, generally seen on fine nights in early summer, that is in the May Term; later in the year he was quickly hidden from view by the thick leaves of the two young chestnuts in the centre of the lawn, and could only be seen at the start and towards the end of his walk. He was also seen sometimes on bright gusty nights in spring and autumn, but with the clouds flying across the moon he would then only be visible for a few instants at a time.

So clear were these apparitions that none of the four witnesses above referred to had any idea but that he was watching a member of the then existing Society taking a walk in the garden. Three of them mentioned the particular college authority they had supposed him to be. Questioned as to how they could have thought this, considering the old-fashioned dress of the figure in the garden, they said the whole appearance was so natural and lifelike that the peculiarities did not strike them until they were asked to describe them. They supposed them to be the mode of dressing for the evenings on the part of the authority they named. He seemed to them to be an old man who might easily wear quaint things. Being asked if they ever saw the figure elsewhere or encountered it on either of the Fellows' Building staircases they all replied in the negative. But G. E. B. said that he

---

[3] This tree was blown down in 1916. Its upturned roots may still be seen.

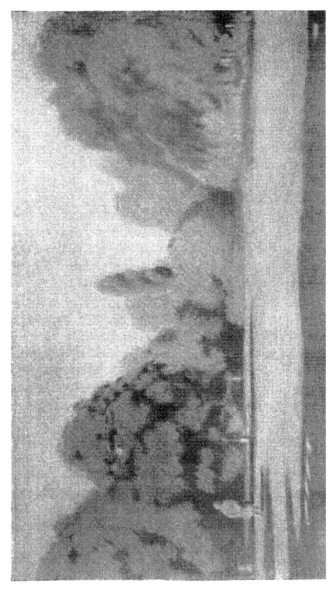

The Fellows' Garden (North View).

"They have observed the figure of a man emerge on the lawn from under the great chestnuts and walk slowly, with bent head, as far as the great yew."

remembered on more than one occasion, after seeing the figure in the garden, he heard, a few minutes later, a ponderous tread mounting slowly to the first floor of his staircase, followed by the sound of the opening and shutting of the door of the rooms where Christopher Round once lived.

*   *   *   *   *   *

Was the figure they alleged that they saw the ghost of Christopher Round? Does he still take the walk which his record tells us he used to take in his lifetime? Does his uneasy spirit dwell upon his deed as in the days of his life here?

This puzzle it is not for me to solve. Like Simon Goodridge, I leave it to the reader, who must judge for himself.

Here is the record and the evidence.

A. P. B.

II

(From the papers collected by Simon Goodridge)

THE RECORD OF CHRISTOPHER ROUND

PART I. INCEPTION

(1)[1]

As I stand here at my tall-boy and look round this dear old panelled room, where so much of my life has been spent, and watch the shadows lengthening in the garden as the sun goes down behind the chestnuts, the feeling comes over me, as it has so often of late, that the time is drawing close when the dim light of my own life will be sinking lower and the twilight be changing to the dark. And with it too comes the thrill of recollection, which such an evening here never fails to bring; the remembrance of that other summer night, so like this in all external things, for here there is little change as the years go by, when occurred that, of which no one else knows the truth, which has over-shadowed my whole life since. It is nearly thirty years ago. I am growing an old man, in a few more years my three score years and ten will be complete, and I am much older than I look or seem. An inward grief that cannot be shared ages a man before his time.

Somehow, too, standing here in the peace of the evening, I feel that in days to come when others live here where I have lived, keeping up the tradition which I have helped to pass on, I should like them to know the truth. If any acts of mine are remembered with praise in that aftertime I think I should like my successors to know all, and then they can continue to remember me thankfully, or to forget me, as they think that I deserve.

---

[1] The divisions into chapters and sections and paragraphs do not occur in the original. They have been introduced for the sake of clearness.

But it is too soon yet for the truth to be known. It must be kept secret until the chance of causing pain to any living person has passed away. I will try and write it down clearly and simply before it is too late, and then, I think, I shall give it to Simon[2] to keep. He is to be trusted, and is one of the few of those who know something of the old days, who are still left.

Why I have come to the decision to do it now is partly because, as I said, I am growing old, partly because of the influence of such an evening on the vividness of one's recollections, and partly because I have looked today, on going through the papers in the bureau over there, between the bedroom and the gyp-room doors, on those two miniatures which I could never bear to show to anyone again. They are excellent likenesses. Philip Collier was, indeed, a handsome fellow, and Mary Clifford looks what she will ever be to me, and what she was, I think, to many, the embodiment of grace and dignity and charity, not of prettiness, but of beauty.

*   *   *   *   *   *

I have copied the above from my diary in which I was writing a few moments ago. It will serve as an introduction to what follows and explain why I am writing it. Now to the matter itself.

(2)

I, Christopher James Round, was born in Derbyshire very nearly seventy years ago. My father was the rector of our village, and I was his third son. My two brothers are dead; one of fever in India in the service of the Company, the other in the wreck of his ship off the coast of Portugal. My elder sister was married to Mr. Bernard Coates, the second son of our squire, and died without children; my younger sister is the wife of Mr. George Verney, the physician in Bedford Square, and has two sons and two daughters. Neither of my brothers married, and when I go our family of Round will be extinct.

I grew up at home, and was well grounded in the Classics by my father, who had been a scholar of Balliol; and, owing to the fact that Mr. Coates, a clergyman and brother of the squire, was living in the village, and was a good mathematician, I received a sound training in that department of

---

[2] Simon Goodridge, Tutor of Christ's College.

science as well. It was early expected that I should receive Holy Orders. I was, I think I may say, much fonder of learning than either of my brothers, one of whom soon went to sea and the other departed for India after a few years at Westminster School. But it seemed strange in some ways that I should be destined for a quiet and scholarly career. I was by far the biggest and most muscular of our family. I stand about six feet in height, and I have been physically a strong man. Yet, if I never felt any great enthusiasm for a clerical career, it was never distasteful, and it pleased my father that one of his sons would be called to his own vocation, and would be likely to remain near him.

In course of time I was sent to Rugby School, where I did well, both in work and in those out-of-door sports for which I was by nature suited.

When the time came for me to proceed to a University my father was inclined to send me to Oxford to his own old College. But the proficiency to which I had attained in Mathematics as well as in Classics, added to the fact that my old tutor at home, Mr. Coates, was a Cambridge man, turned the scale in favour of this place, where nearly all my life since has been spent. Accordingly I was sent up to Trinity College to obtain a Scholarship. It was my first visit to Cambridge, and I was lodged in Trinity Street over the shop of Mr. Ferrier,[1] clockmaker, in rooms where Mr. Coates had kept in his time.

It was on the second day of my stay that the first incident occurred that I have to relate. On that day I first met Philip Collier, with whom my future was to be so strangely bound up, whose history, with my own, forms the subject of these papers.

I was sitting in the public room of the Blue Boar, drinking a glass of wine and reading one of the books on which I expected to be questioned, when I became aware of laughter and chattering going on behind me. It was evidently the host's daughter engaged in conversation with a man, and a young man, but from where I was sitting I could not see them. What attracted me then, as it was to do so often in years to come, was the exceeding pleasant quality of the man's voice. Youthful, gay and sweet, with a rich and delicate intonation, even in careless talk it was a sound never to be forgotten. I heard it for some time, and then, curiosity getting the better of me, I turned my chair, and, on the excuse of asking for my

---

[1] This shop has disappeared. It stood on the site now occupied by the Union of London and Smith's Bank.

glass to be refilled, I looked straight across to where the speakers stood. I can see the scene as if it had been yesterday. Rachel (I came to know her well in after days and to like her for the merry, honest, kindly girl and woman she was) was leaning on the high back of a chair, a small table was in front of her. Supporting one arm on the settle in a pose of easy elegance was a man of my own age. I saw Philip Collier for the first time, and at the same instant he looked across at me and our eyes met. I have often wondered since whether there was a prophecy contained in the fact of our first meeting in a public hostelry, with the wine on the table in front of us and a woman between.

My glass was refilled by Rachel, and while she was so occupied Collier (to give him his name, which, of course, I then did not know) sat down and began to draw on a piece of paper which he took from his pocket. Rachel left the room; neither of us spoke, and after I had read a little further in my book I saw Collier tear up his paper, take his hat and go out. I followed soon afterwards, having an appointment with the College examiners. So ended our first meeting. I was successful in the matter of the Scholarship, and spent some weeks at home before entering into residence at Trinity.

(3)

My first year at Trinity passed uneventfully, and it was not until my fourth term that I met Collier again. In that term I received an invitation to dine with the Tutor of St. John's College, who was a friend of Mr. Coates, my tutor at home. We dined in his rooms in the second court at St. John's, and amongst the other guests was Philip Collier, to whom I was introduced. I remember that it was a very pleasant meal, and that it owed much of its success to the attractive manners and personality of Collier himself. Though, as I discovered, only a scholar of St. John's in his second year (for he, too, had been sitting for a Scholarship when we first met), he had already made an impression upon his contemporaries and was a great favourite with the dons. Once again I was struck with his beautiful voice and gallant presence. He was as tall as myself, but looked taller, for he was lither and much more lightly built. He had golden hair, which curled brightly over his head, and clear eyes of a very dark blue. As I came to know afterwards, his strength was very great, much exceeding that which he appeared to possess, and he excelled in feats of physical agility and endurance. But our acquaintance for some time remained of the slightest.

As time went on I gained good opinions from my tutors as to my abilities, and developed a real interest in my studies, and it was suggested that I should enter for the Bell Scholarship, which is looked upon as one of the early undergraduate honours. My Tutor told me that there were not many candidates, and, in discussing those who were likely to be my rivals, I remember that he said, "There is a Scholar of St. John's who may be dangerous. His name is Collier, and Brunell (the best classical 'coach' of those days) says he is one of the most brilliant pupils that he has had."

I worked very hard for the Scholarship, and was much disappointed when the result was announced and I found that Collier and another man were bracketed equal first and I was only honourably mentioned. It was the first of the long series of contests in which Collier and I were matched with each other, in which he always beat me by slender margins, which made defeat all the more exasperating. And yet looking back, with the judgment that comes with years, I can say deliberately, and without malice or conceit, that I know I was the sounder scholar of the two. I was better read, I was more conscientious, I was more intellectually original. But I lacked the facility, the grace, and, above all, the appearance of doing work without effort, which enabled Philip Collier to impress his examiners and contemporaries so much.

As terms passed I entered for further University distinctions, such as the Browne Scholarship and Medals, and each time Collier entered too, and each time he beat me by a little and carried off the prize, while I had to be content with monotonous honourable mention. Only once, in the Craven Scholarship, did I succeed, and then we were placed together first.

The affair began to weigh upon my mind; it seemed useless to try to gain those honours which go a long way towards making a successful academic career. And I was now set upon making the University my permanent home, and was deeply interested in my work, and the prospect pleased my father. Moreover, my College authorities spoke well of me, and I was almost uniformly successful in gaining all the College distinctions that were open to undergraduates. But I was anxious to acquire a good reputation in the University at large and the constant running second to Collier annoyed me. It injured my pride, and I felt that it lowered me in the eyes of my tutors.

At length the time came when we entered for the Mathematical Tripos. Although the Classics were my especial care, I was anxious to obtain a good place in Mathematics, and I could not help feeling curiosity as to how my rival would fare. His honours so far had all been Classical ones. When the list appeared I found that I was fifteenth Wrangler, which was satisfactory enough, and I received much congratulation; but through it all, though I knew I had done well, I was conscious that the greatest glow of satisfaction was caused by the knowledge that Collier was placed twenty-first. I had beaten him unmistakably on this occasion, and, unworthy though the feeling of elation may have been, I think it was humanly excusable.

I set to work with redoubled energy at my Classical studies and made the first of my publications. This, however, only resulted in another blow. Collier produced a small book about the same time, and attracted more attention by his grace of style than I did by scholarship. We both took first classes in the Classical Tripos, being bracketed second to another Trinity man, and proceeded to our degrees soon after.

So ended our undergraduate careers, leaving me with a feeling of disappointment and annoyance in spite of my successes.

(4)

It was a strange thing, considering the life that we led here in those days that Collier and I encountered each other so seldom in social intercourse. Our rivalry made us pretty well acquainted, but we seldom met in the rooms of other undergraduates or in those of the Fellows. I frequently encountered him on the road riding to Newmarket, or to Huntingdon, and I remember once falling in with some undergraduates near Royston and having a great race home, and that he was one of the party. Once, too, at the end of term I travelled to London with him on the same coach. But our meetings were few and far between, and we knew little of each other; but from other people I was aware that he was a leader in his own College and a favourite in University society generally.

My career so far had justified me in hoping to obtain a Fellowship at Trinity. This in due course came about. My ordination was a great pleasure to my father, and took place at Ely, and on the same day, at the same place, Philip Collier was ordained too. He had become a Classical lecturer at St. John's, and then had been offered a Fellowship. So we were both launched on our academic careers, and very soon we came into collision again. This was a curious chance, and revived some of the bitterness that I had formerly felt.

The Public Orator, whose duty it was to compose and deliver Latin orations on stated occasions, was taken ill, and it was necessary to appoint someone in his place for a term at least. Various persons were approached, but the conditions insisted upon by the Orator, that if he set aside part of his emolument for the payment of a deputy he should be allowed to inspect the draft orations of this person, gave great offence. None of his seniors, or equals in standing, would consent, and the post thus came within the reach of comparatively junior persons. Those desiring the post were requested to submit specimen orations to the Orator, whose recommendation would be followed by ratification by the Vice-Chancellor. The post was a tempting one for younger Masters of Arts who were Fellows, and desirous of acquiring standing in the University. I, with many others, submitted orations in draft form, and I was gratified at being one of four selected by the Orator to declaim before him and the Vice-Chancellor. Collier was another, and I soon saw that I had no chance. In grace, diction and bearing he far surpassed us other three, and was appointed without difficulty. Once again I had suffered defeat from him, for I knew I had little to fear from the others. I believe he acquitted himself well while he held the post; but it was characteristic of his easy-going nature that the Public Orator, a dull but precise personage, was often scandalised by careless mistakes in the drafts submitted to him.

(5)

I was a Fellow of Trinity for a few years, but it soon became evident that it would be difficult for me to obtain a College office there, and I was anxious to find a position at one of the smaller Colleges where there might be a greater opening.

During these years I heard little of Collier. He gave up his Fellowship at St. John's from some difficulty, I believe, about his theological views and went abroad, and spent a long time in Italy, chiefly in Venice. It was then I presume that he acquired that mastery of Italian which made him celebrated as a speaker of that beautiful tongue. In after years I often heard him sing Italian songs with a grace and truthfulness that I think few non-Italian singers can have equalled.

The chance for which I had been looking arrived at last. Through two
College livings falling vacant, and two deaths, there happened to be a
number of elections imminent at Christ's College. I had friends there, and
was informed that one of the Fellowships might be given to me if I cared to
accept it. This I intimated my willingness to do.

While matters were in course of negotiation I was surprised one day, in
walking up King's Parade, to encounter Collier. He was looking handsomer
than ever, and was evidently in the best of spirits. He told me that he was
lodging at the Lion Inn, and that he would be pleased if I would come there
and take a glass of wine with him. This I did, and, in course of conversation,
he said he was weary of wandering and, hearing that there was a chance of
obtaining a post again in Cambridge, he had returned to look for it. He did
not say what the post was. He was very entertaining, and gave me beautiful
and graphic accounts of his journeys in Italy, Corsica and Sicily, in the
course of which he had visited many places, then little known to
Englishmen. We parted on good terms. The old jealousy and grudge I had
felt had been dispelled by his removal from Cambridge life, and I no longer
looked upon him as a successful rival, but as one who had left the academic
fold. I had done some good work during the last few years, and knew that
my reputation was advancing, while Collier's, which at the first seemed to
be eclipsing my own, now scarcely existed. I had paid little serious attention
to his statement that he was thinking of settling in Cambridge again. I was
soon to be rudely awakened.

About two weeks after our meeting the elections at Christ's took place,
and I became a Fellow there, together with Owen, of St. John's, who was
elected on the same day. Owing to the deaths and removals that had
occurred there were many rooms vacant, and I had the unusual good
fortune, for a new Fellow, of being offered a set on the first floor in the
Fellows' Building. It is generally agreed, I think, that they are amongst the
most beautiful not only at Christ's, but in the University as a whole.[1] I
occupied them with great pleasure, and have lived in them ever since, and
stand writing in them now. The beautiful panelling, the dignity of the
whole apartment, with its gracious view of the Second Court, though in

---

[1] This set of rooms is on Staircase A. They are well known to many Cambridge
men, for they were occupied for many years by the present Master of Christ's,
Dr. A. E. Shipley. They are now occupied by Mr. Norman McLean, Senior
Tutor.

my earliest days the latter was different from what it is now,[2] the peaceful outlook on our beautiful garden, have always endeared my rooms to me. The charm I felt when I first entered them has remained with me till today, and though the tragedy of which I have to write is so closely connected with the garden, even it has never entirely deprived me of pleasure in my immediate surroundings. Perhaps it should have filled them with horror, but it has steeped them in melancholy and calm. Yet there is one part of the garden into which I shall never go again. Since that night I have never penetrated beyond the great yew, or into the garden house. What lies beyond has been a forbidden scene for nearly thirty years.

I had entered upon my duties at Christ's with great pleasure, but my unspoiled happiness was soon past. At one of the first College meetings that I attended the question of filling one of the remaining vacancies among the Fellows was discussed, and to my great surprise I found that Philip Collier's name had already been put forward. I felt instinctively that I would rather not have him in the same Society as myself; I did not desire the past rivalry and defeat to be repeated in the Society of which I was now a permanent member. Somehow I felt conclusively that Collier and I would come into collision, and that he would carry the day. But I could do nothing. There was nothing to urge against his election. His career had been brilliant in the extreme, and he had been able to give satisfactory explanations of the reason why he had left St. John's. It appeared that he had wished to assure himself definitely of his theological views and had done so, and it seemed to redound to his credit that while he had had any doubts he had scrupled to go on holding his Fellowship. Also it was alleged that he had spent his time in Italy in much antiquarian research, though of this I can honestly say I never found proof. However, I could not make objection to a man who had obviously proved himself superior to me in our undergraduate contests and the matter rapidly went through. I understood that the Tutor and Dean of that time were the two persons who had done most to secure for him his election. They had both known him in past days, and he shared some of their views. He was elected and admitted less

---

[2] The low building called "Rats' Hall" formerly stretched across the Second Court, parallel with the Fellows' Building. It must have been demolished about the time of which Round writes. The present building at the side of the Second Court was then erected.

than a month after I had become a member of the Society. We were both College lecturers.

Thus began that rivalry of nearly ten years which spoiled my early life here, and ended in the tragedy which has haunted it ever since.

(6)

Those ten years will always be looked back to with pleasure by Christ's men. It was a very pleasant Society here, and the College more than held its own. Our undergraduate members were excellent young men, and their successes were of a gratifying nature. Though it does not lie with me to make the statement, I know that much of this success was due to Collier and myself. We both brought many pupils to Christ's, and each of us had a reputation as a teacher which was becoming recognised at the Schools and in the University. We each published books that won attention. As time went on I began to realise the pleasure of at last getting the better of Collier. So far he had beaten me in everything; but my pupils were generally the better grounded, and their achievements were of a more satisfactory kind. This I know gave me some consolation for the former defeats, but in other ways Collier still surpassed me in a way that kept alive the old soreness. He was the life and soul of our Society, and was very popular on all social occasions and with our numerous guests. His rooms were crowded with people, and he was a graceful host; he paid many visits, and his system of entertaining must have cost him large sums of money. In spite of the want of soundness in his work, his reputation academically and socially grew. We were frequently in opposition in matters of College business, and, though I can assert with a clear mind that I was often in the right, he seldom failed to carry the day by his charm of manner and winning personality. Collier was one of the favourites of the gods, and I have always been, I fear a dull dog.

THE RECORD OF CHRISTOPHER ROUND

PART II.   DEVELOPMENT

(1)

It was after affairs had gone on in the manner I have described for about four years that I met Mary Clifford. My friend Henderson, of Pembroke, possessed a villa on the Lake of Geneva. He asked me to spend part of the Long Vacation there with him and his sister. We first travelled by post-chaise across France, and altogether had a most enjoyable tour. My stay on the Lake was a somewhat prolonged one, and it was about ten days before I left that Mary Clifford came to consult Mr. Henderson as to some of her late husband's papers. I had heard of her before, because part of my own studies had been on the same lines as those of Sir Henry Clifford. The latter had once been British Minister at Berne, and was an excellent scholar. He had been dead about three years when Mary Clifford came to the Hendersons. She was engaged in editing his papers, and Henderson was helping her over some of the difficulties.

I will not stay long to describe Mary Clifford. She was the daughter of the famous Archdeacon Champneys, and inherited much of his breadth of mind and physical grace. Not much over middle height, she had the most beautiful carriage and the greatest simplicity and dignity of manner that I have ever seen in a woman. Her brow and eyes were perhaps her greatest charm, and her expression of candour and loving kindness moved all hearts towards her at the first sight. Her hair was simply braided, and her costume was always graceful and generally black, in keeping with her position as a widow. She was possessed of a most cultivated mind, and had an excellent judgment and literary taste. In short, Mary Clifford was a beautiful, good, and very gentle woman. She was possessed of an ample fortune, partly left to her by her father and partly by her husband, and she had no children. She must have been a little more than thirty when we first met.

We became well acquainted during those happy days near Geneva, and there were many questions connected with her husband's papers in which I was able to assist her and Henderson. Before I left she expressed the hope that we should meet in London. I returned to my work in Cambridge, and did not see her again for nearly a year. Then, at Henderson's request, I went to her in London about some fresh papers of her husband's that she was preparing for the press. At this time I saw her, at her cousin's house in Bedford Square, nearly every other day for more than a month, and, though I was unaware of it at the time, her society and conversation became the chief pleasure of my life. It may easily be judged then with what joy I received the news that after another tour abroad she hoped to return to England and settle down to see the proofs of her husband's literary works through the press, and that, for the purpose of consulting Mr. Henderson and others, among whom she was kind enough to name myself, she purposed to take a house in or near Cambridge.

How I looked forward to her coming I need not dwell upon here. The prospect of it quite removed my mind from the petty difficulties of College life and helped me to surmount them with an ease that surprised myself. For I am by nature, I fear, heavy-minded and apt to take seriously what others throw lightly aside. Even my secret rivalry with Collier ceased to be annoying, and seemed less important; all the more so as I had a comforting feeling that Collier had come near the end of his capabilities as a scholar. Although giving occasional flashes of brilliancy his work was becoming uncertain and perfunctory, and he seemed more and more immersed in social gaieties. But he was still very popular, and any falling off that there might be was not apparent to other eyes.

But my expectations were for a time doomed to disappointment. Lady Clifford went to France and Italy, and it was nearly a year before she returned to England. The delay was due to her contracting a form of blood-poisoning at Genoa. After her return she was detained in London by family business, and then by the illness of her cousin, so that it was nearly two years since our work together in London before she was free to carry out her intention and settle temporarily near Cambridge. The long delay made her advent all the more welcome.

I heard from the Hendersons that she had taken the Manor House at Chesterton, and about the beginning of the October term she began her residence there. I soon had the felicity of seeing her again, and at her especial request I arranged to pay regular visits to the Manor to make headway with the mass of literary material that had to be gone through. It was a delightful occupation.

For the greater part of a year I spent two or three afternoons in each week at the Manor, and the memory of those hours is the most cherished recollection that I have. Lady Clifford was always kind, always gentle, and really interested in our work. Long before the year was past and the first part of our task was finished I was aware that the crisis of my life had come, that some day I should be compelled to put my fortunes to the test and ask her hand in marriage. It would mean the end of my College career if she consented, for my Fellowship lapsed if I married, but that weighed not with me at all, with me to whom heretofore my College life and advancement in my academic career had been all in all. I had inherited some private means from my mother, which had been increased by the deaths of my brothers. I looked eagerly for a sign that my feelings were in any measure returned.

(2)

Such was the state of affairs when the first year of Lady Clifford's residence at the Manor at Chesterton ended, and she spent nearly six months in foreign travel. During her stay near Cambridge she had mixed to some extent in the County and University society, though she apparently cared little for gaiety, and lived very quietly with the cousin who acted as her companion. Yet many of the University residents had made her acquaintance, though none of my friends at Christ's knew her well. I had been the means of introducing one or two of them to her, but I had never been inclined to make opportunities for them to meet her.

I waited in a fever of impatience for her return, and was delighted to find how easily we renewed our old pleasant ways of friendship.

We had pursued our work for a few weeks, and my hopes were becoming stronger, when one afternoon, by a casual remark, she dissipated the feeling of peace and security which I had enjoyed for so long.

I remember it quite well.

We were sitting in the pleasant library of the Manor, a comparatively small room with long windows opening on to the lawn. The sun shone in brightly, and there was a view over the garden and through the poplars and willows to the streak of the river beyond. We had just put aside a pile of papers which we had read through, when she leaned back in her high chair by the writing table and told me she would have to cease work for that day, as she had notes to write before going out; among her correspondents, she added, was a friend of mine, Mr. Philip Collier.

I can remember distinctly the stab at the heart which the mention of this name gave me and the sense of foreboding which her words caused me. I cannot say why, but I had instinctively refrained from introducing Collier to Mary Clifford, and I was not aware that they knew each other. She went on to explain that she had met Mr. Collier in Italy during her last tour, and that she had been struck with his mastery of Italian. With other friends she was asking him to dine with her. I said little in reply and walked home moodily.

The dinner I suppose took place, but I did not hear Collier mentioned again for some time; indeed, the next notice I had of his acquaintance with Lady Clifford came from Philip Collier himself. He was showing some of the Fellows in the Combination Room a book of Italian poems he was about to publish, and I heard him say that he was taking them to-morrow to show to Lady Clifford.

From that time my happiness gradually vanished. Not that Lady Clifford was any less kind to me, our work progressed in the same even way, but I saw with chagrin the growth of the friendship that sprang up between her and Collier. They were both interested in Italian, and read and discussed together, so that in a short time Collier was as much at the Manor as I was, and I could not help seeing that he was regarded with increasing interest and favour.

For a year things went on in this way. Collier appeared to take his friendship with her very much for granted as he took all his success in life.

Then three things happened which brought matters to a crisis and led up to the tragedy which destroyed one life, eventually I think caused the end of another, and ruined all the happiness of a third.

THE RECORD OF CHRISTOPHER ROUND

PART III. CULMINATION

(1)

For some terms it had been a matter of remark among the Fellows that Collier was becoming less sociable. I remember what a pang it gave me when our Bursar jestingly suggested that he must be in love. But on thinking over the change in his habits I noted that it dated from before his meeting with Lady Clifford. On this point therefore I was somewhat reassured. But that there was an alteration in Collier I was certain. He would not receive company after nine o'clock if he could help it, and yet formerly he had liked to have his rooms crowded until all hours of the night. He "kept" on the first floor room in the Fellows' Building at the Christ's Pieces end.[1] Also he would disappear of an afternoon and give no account of whither his excursions had lain.

It was in the early part of the year which would complete our tenth at Christ's, and the third since Lady Clifford had first come to Cambridge, and just over a year since Collier had first begun to visit her, when I received one evening an urgent message from the brother of one of Collier's friends who was ill. Mr. Phillips, who was also a friend of mine, said he had been unable to find Collier, and would I kindly give him a message from his sick friend, without fail, during the evening. I promised to do so.

I went to Collier's rooms at nine and again at ten-thirty, but each time found his oak sported. As the matter was urgent I went again at midnight, though with reluctance, as I knew that Collier had stated that he disliked being disturbed late in the evening.

To my relief I found the outer door open. I knocked on the inner one, and a voice I scarcely recognised bade me come in. What followed gave

---

[1] This set of rooms is on Staircase B. They are now occupied by Mr. C. R. Fay, Fellow of the College.

me one of the severest shocks I have ever suffered. For I liked Collier as a man, and, had he not crossed my path so often, my feelings towards him would have been warmly friendly.

The rooms he occupied are very handsome, the panelling runs up nearly to the ceiling, and the four windows are beautifully set. There is a wide arched stone fireplace. As I entered the room was lit by a lamp on the centre table; the shade was all awry and a beam shone across the room, which was otherwise in semi-darkness. The streak of light marked out the fireplace in which the fire was burning low.

In a chair in front of it, one of those high-backed railed chairs then so usual in Fellows' rooms, sat Philip Collier. His arms hung limply over the arms of the chair. When I apologised for intruding he turned his face towards me in the light, and I was struck with the foolish expression of his normally alert features. His eyes looked dim. I gave my message, noticing that he did not, with his usual pleasant courtesy, ask me to take a chair. He made no reply, nor even looked at me. Thinking there must be something wrong, or that I may have only half awaked him from sleep, for he looked fatigued, and his boots were covered with wet soil, I went to his side, when he suddenly smote me with his hand in a purposeless way and gave what sounded like a thick, gurgling laugh. At the same time I caught a strong smell of spirits. The truth dawned upon me, Collier was helplessly drunk.

I confess that I was staggered. There was nothing unusual in a gentleman being drunk in those days, but Collier, like the majority of us at Christ's, was notably moderate in his use of wine. Moreover, it was not wine, with the odour of which I, like most Cambridge residents, was well acquainted, but spirits. Gentlemen in those times did not become drunk on spirits, and if they drank too much wine, usually did so after dinner, or in company with each other. Collier's dress showed that he had not been dining. He was dressed as if for a country walk.

Seeing that he was in no condition to receive my message, and that he was quite safe in his chair, I withdrew.

As I left I closed the outer oak of the rooms. On reaching the half-landing I chanced to look up, and to my surprise observed that this door was swinging open. Hastily I retraced my steps, thinking that I had failed to shut it properly, for I felt that Collier should not be seen by anyone in his present condition. I pushed the door to again, and then discovered that some of the screws in the lock had worn loose, and that when the

"The shade was all awry and a beam shone across the room."

draught caught the door the lock gave and the door easily came open. It was now apparent how it was that it had been unfastened when I came up. With my knife I succeeded in tightening the screws sufficiently to hold the door fairly securely, and, having closed it, I descended once more.

On returning to my rooms I retired for the night, but could not sleep. I kept turning over in my mind the sight I had just witnessed. It made clear to me why Collier withdrew from society and so often shut himself up of an evening. The erratic nature of much of his work for a long time past was also explained, but there were two things that puzzled me. First, there were no signs of bottles or glasses in Collier's rooms, except the usual decanters on his sideboard. Secondly, his dress and the thick black soil on his boots, which had left their traces on the stairs, showed that he had recently been out-of-doors. What I did not understand was how he had returned to his rooms. He could not have come in at the great gate and crossed the courts in his condition without exciting comment. The question that puzzled me was how had he returned without observation. That he had so returned I was sure, for shortly before going to his rooms I had had occasion to go to the gate and, on asking the porter if Mr. Collier had come into College, was told that he had not come in, nor had he been seen to go out during the evening. He must, therefore, have returned by some private way; by which also he had gone out, unless he had been away since the afternoon.

Not many days afterwards I found the clue.

It had always been my custom to walk in the garden at all seasons. In the spring and summer I am fond of doing so in the evenings when the night has closed in. The curves of the trees against the darkening sky and the line of the Fellows' Building always please me, and the softness of the lawn and the quiet stirring of the leaves of the chestnuts along the old wall are soothing after a hard period of work.

One evening, less than a month after the discovery of which I have just written, I was sauntering on the lower lawn, beside Milton's mulberry tree, later than usual. It must have been at least nine o'clock. It was peculiarly still, and there was scarcely a sound to be heard. Just as I reached the path by the high wall, which forms the end of the garden, my ear caught the noise of crackling, as though someone was snapping twigs under foot.

I listened again and heard a noise as of a body forcing its way through bushes. I turned to find what it was, and walked quickly round the shrubs which edge the swimming bath in the north-east corner of the garden. The sound I had heard was repeated, and seemed to come from beside the

THE FELLOWS' GARDEN (SOUTH VIEW).

"The figure of a man crossed a patch of comparative light on the darkness of the lawn."

garden house at the head of the bath. I walked to that end along the edge of the bath and went through the house and on to the path at the end of the great lawn.

Just as I did so the figure of a man crossed a patch of comparative light on the darkness of the lawn.

I immediately recognised Collier; there was no mistaking his tall, athletic form. He was walking quickly, but unsteadily, and brushed more than once against the bushes at the edge of the bed. At length he reached the broad path at the head of the garden, and seemed as if about to enter the arched way that leads under the Fellows' Building to the gate. Instead, he turned suddenly aside and made for the end of the building by Christ's Pieces. There is a little-used gate[1] there which leads into the Second Court from the garden, and is only a few paces from Collier's staircase. In a few moments I heard the gate click, and, after waiting a little while, saw a light in Collier's rooms. That he was again intoxicated I felt sure. I left the garden and went up his stairs. His door was sported.

The next day, having occasion to be in the garden in the forenoon with the Dean, who was our Garden Steward, I took the opportunity, after I had left him, to inspect the narrow path and shrubbery on the further side of the bath, along which Collier must have come. This path is scarcely used except by the gardeners, and leads to a door, which opens on to the end of Christ's Pieces near to King Street. This door is seldom opened except to bring in material for the garden, or to take out refuse. The path is very narrow, and is bordered by soft soil covered with rough shrubs. Looking about I saw that there were footmarks in this soil, and that they began quite close to the gate as though someone had entered and then found it difficult to keep to the path.

Collier's method of coming into College was now explained. As a Fellow he would have a key which fitted this door, as well as the gate of the garden, by which I had seen him gain the Second Court. He could then get back to his rooms and shut himself in without anyone knowing that he had been out at all. The distance from the garden gate, leading into the court, to his rooms is, as I said, only a few paces, and no one passes that way. His rooms are on the first floor, so that he was not likely to meet

---

[1] This gate still exists. It is in the railings between the end of the Fellows' Building and the railings running along Christ's Piece, close to the door leading from the Second Court to the Piece.

anyone on the stairs during the short time it took him to mount them. The real reason of his early retirement at night was now apparent.

I was much puzzled to know if I should mention to Collier what I had seen, or not. I was sorry for him, as I would be for any man of brilliant parts who was going the way to ruin. But I had gained my information by an accident, and did not consider that it gave me a right to approach him.

Not long after this happened the second event which I have to describe.

(2)

In spite of the habits in which I now knew him to indulge, there was little outward change in Collier. Much to my chagrin I found that he and Mary Clifford were seeing more and more of each other. Their intimacy, or what was thought to be such, began to attract attention, and, although my own friendship with Lady Clifford continued in its old way, I was sensible that there was no progress towards warmer feelings, as I had hoped might be the case. For some time we had appeared to be drawn more together, but now all seemed to be stationary, and I could not but attribute my lack of success to the attraction exercised by Collier. He was constantly at the Manor.

One day shortly after my adventure in the garden I went to Collier's rooms on a matter of business. It was about ten in the morning, and the sun was beginning to flood his beautiful sitting-room. He was standing in a beam of sunlight, and was looking his best, upright and handsome, with a merry smile lurking in the corners of his mouth and in his eyes. It was difficult to believe that he could be the same man that I had seen a few weeks before huddled drunkenly in the armchair by the fire. He bade me cheerily good day, and then, without a sign of embarrassment, he suddenly turned to a leathern box which was lying open on the table in front of us.

"What do you think of these?" he asked.

I will give Philip Collier the credit that is his due. He never had any idea of the feelings I entertained for Mary Clifford. But the things he showed me sent a cold shiver through me, and I had difficulty in replying. In the box were two miniatures very finely executed. One was a speaking likeness of Mary Clifford, radiant and beautiful, and the other, which was not quite finished, was an excellent portrait of Philip Collier himself. I expressed my admiration, and enquired who was the artist. Collier threw back his head and laughed happily.

"Why, I am," he said, "or rather I and Mary—Lady Clifford, I mean—together."

I was dumbfounded : not only by the fact of the paintings, but by the easy confidence of his tone and by the slip he had made in his reference to Mary Clifford.

It transpired from what he told me that miniature painting had been one of his many accomplishments, that he had revived it during his last visit to Italy, and had been instructing Lady Clifford, who herself knew much of the art. Without realising the pain he was giving he dwelt on the difficulties they had surmounted together. Hers, he said, had been easier, as he had done most of it himself, but his she had, apparently, insisted on really helping with, and, he said, it was difficult for him to paint himself. They hoped soon to finish it, and then he was to keep hers and she his.

The incident made me wretchedly unhappy. He had made matters worse by saying that Lady Clifford would not mind our discussing the miniatures, as there was no secret about them, and many friends had seen them working at them. But I knew that the worst had befallen. Mary Clifford would not give her portrait to a man and accept his in return unless she was really attracted by him. Knowing her as I did I felt that an exchange of gifts of this nature signified an intimate attachment, such as that for which I had vainly hoped.

I said little to Collier, but every day I sat and brooded in my rooms on his perpetual good fortune and on my own failures. And ever and anon, as I thought, there came over me a feeling of hatred and disgust as that other picture came back to me, of an oak-walled room and a drunken figure sitting helpless in the gleam of the lamplight.

Needless to say, my work suffered from this pre-occupation, which was doubly unfortunate, for just then, as I shall show presently, it was important that my work should be of the best; and also Philip Collier, apparently owing to the inspiration he derived from his association with Mary Clifford, was in one of his most brilliant moods. All our friends noticed it, and one evening in the Combination Room, when Collier was making the company round the table merry with his wit, old Dr. Caleb Parkins, our Bursar, who was sitting next to me, and was never very discreet in his remarks, said in my ear,

"Collier is in form to-night."

I assented.

"Effects of successful love-making, I suppose," went on old Caleb.

"What do you mean?" I asked.

"Why everyone knows that he goes courting at the Manor at Chesterton, and that the fair citadel is on the point of capitulating."

I was too heartsick to reply. So it had come to this, that Collier was recognised as the successful suitor of Mary Clifford.

My wrath at having her name bandied about in gossip was, I fear, lost in the self-pity and anger I felt at my own defeat. Whichever way I turned there seemed no escape from Collier and his successes. I brooded more and more over the triumphs he had enjoyed in the past, and the still worse one I saw looming ahead. All chance for me was gone, I could see that, although Mary Clifford was as kind as ever. But I could seldom bear to go to the Manor. I grew more and more morose and solitary. I tramped the country roads and took my lonely perambulations in the garden, thinking all the while of Collier's victory and horrified at the idea of its coming to a man addicted, as I knew him to be, to secret drunkenness.

The gloom from which I suffered thus became aggravated and affected my work still more, which may have been partly responsible for the third incident that befell about this time.

(3)

The old Professor of Greek had recently retired. Cambridge Professors are a long-lived race, and the holder of the Chair of Greek had been no exception to the rule. Professor Philpotts was at least eighty-five, and he had outlived many of his contemporaries who were better scholars than he. To the men of a generation junior to himself, who were teachers of his subject, he had a rooted objection, and he had made matters so unpleasant for these would-be supplanters, (as he regarded them), that most of them had been glad to accept ecclesiastical preferment and make their careers elsewhere. In consequence, when the Professor spoke of retiring, it was nearly certain that his influence, which was great, would bring about the appointment of a man much younger than himself. Among his favourite pupils had been both Philip Collier and myself, and both of us entered as candidates for the Professorship. Somewhat to the surprise of us both, and entirely to that of most of our friends, it became known that our names were favourably regarded. This was almost entirely due to Dr. Philpotts and his determination to prevent the election of any of the senior University Lecturers. Many of them were, I believe, of second-rate ability, and their claims were easily defeated by the argument that the chair should be filled by someone young and energetic; a plea which Dr. Philpotts himself advanced with unblushing effrontery. The outcome of all these manœuvres was that excitement waxed hot in inner academic circles as to whether Collier or I would be elected. Dr. Philpotts was a great talker, and there was little secrecy about the whole matter. It was generally held, I think, that mine was the better chance. My scholarship, I can say without fear of challenge, was sounder than Collier's, and the expert scholars who constituted the electors were not likely to be led away by Collier's more superficial brilliance. It naturally was not a matter on which wagers could be laid in our College Combination Room, so that no record of them will be found in the wine-book, but, privately, I believe there was much betting on the result. Dr. Philpotts was understood to lean towards me, so that the odds were in my favour.

I was anxious to be successful, for it would be a crowning step in my academic career to gain such a position at the age I was then; but my pre-occupation with the relationship of Collier and Mary Clifford and the catastrophe, as I felt it to be, that was impending, prevented me from paying proper attention to the matter. As I have said, my work suffered from the abstraction of my thoughts, and a course of lectures which I was delivering in the University failed to make the mark that I think they would otherwise have done. This was especially unfortunate in view of the succession to the Professorship.

It was a few weeks after the affair of the miniatures that I was surprised one day to receive a call from Dr. Philpotts. That great man seldom troubled to go and see anyone. After some polite conversation he intimated the reason for his call. There was, he said, much doubt as to the appointment of his successor; he, personally, would have liked to see me appointed, and he had pressed my claims in the right quarter. I ventured to thank him. Unfortunately, Dr. Philpotts went on to inform me, Dr. Cookson, the great Oxford scholar, had recently been staying in Cambridge, and had not been favourably impressed with the course of lectures I was delivering. Moreover, having the pleasure of knowing Lady Clifford, he had often visited her house, and had been much struck with the scholarship and freshness of outlook of Mr. Collier, whom he met there. Dr. Cookson had been consulted by many of the electors, and had expressed his opinion strongly. This, Dr. Philpotts said, had practically settled the matter in Collier's favour, and he had come to tell me so himself, thinking I would prefer to be prepared for the announcement, which would be made in a few days. I managed to thank him and ushered him out, but when he was gone I fell a prey to the blackest anger and despair.

I knew that Collier intended me no evil, but intended or not, his career blighted mine. He had spoiled my undergraduate record and often defeated me in matters of College business, but these were small things compared with what had happened now. Not only was he gaining a position which would make him far beyond me in academic standing and give him a precedence even in College which stopped all hopes of much further advancement for me; for the Professorship at his early age meant that he would probably be the future Head of our House if he wished; but, worst of all, he had come between me and the woman I loved, who, but for him, would, I believe, have come to entertain a regard for me.

What made it all the more galling was that the loss of the Professorship was due to the failure of my love affair, and his success in the one was due to his success in the other. I had no doubt that it was the stimulus of Mary Clifford's society that had made him so brilliant that he had produced such an impression on Dr. Cookson. With the same helpful influence I could have been brilliant too.

Moreover, the Professorship made it more possible for him to marry Mary Clifford. Without it the loss of his Fellowship would have meant that he must ask her to be married to a penniless scholar, and Collier was too proud a man to do that easily, or else he would have had to take a College living, which would have ended his academic career. That step at least would have given me the consolation of his removal from Cambridge. But the Professorship would give him the means to marry and yet to continue to live in Cambridge. Could I bear to put up with that? To live solitary, defeated and forlorn in my rooms and to see Collier, gay and successful, having domestically and academically all I had ever hoped for and should never have? I felt it was past human endurance. Then beside it all was the thought that the man was unworthy. That, in spite of his brilliancy and good manners, he was rotten underneath, addicted secretly to a vice that must not only ruin his career and bring disgrace on the offices he would hold, but cause bitter sorrow and humiliation to the woman I loved. And I could do nothing to prevent it.

Tortured by these thoughts I dragged out a miserable existence, keeping aloof from my colleagues and doing little work. I could not sleep. The whole affair became an obsession and preyed upon my mind to the

.

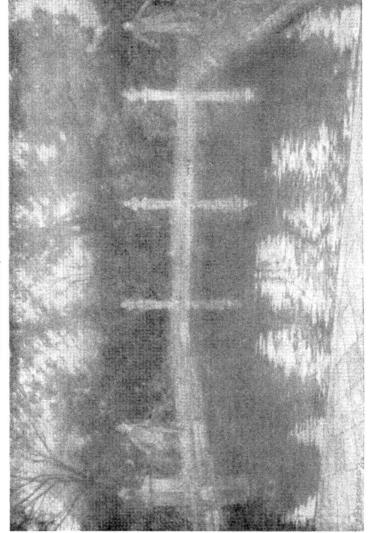

The Swimming Bath, Fellows' Garden.

exclusion of all else. Not caring to read I prolonged my night walks in the garden, sometimes until the night was late. The coolness of the night air, the softness of the lawns, the gentle swaying of the trees, were a soothing influence even in the torture I was then enduring. I used to walk round and round the garden, by way of the path, on the left, under the great chestnuts, and then out on to the lawn and past the great yew and the weeping ash and by the grass path on to the lower lawn, round Milton's tree, and then by the bathing pool back to the great lawn again under the copper beech tree. How many times I would make this round I could not say. I lost count of time, and was almost in a state of semi-consciousness.

This was my case on the night when the tragedy happened that has darkened my life ever since.

(4)

It was a beautiful night, calm and still, with a little moon and brilliant stars; I had perambulated the garden as usual until I think it must have been near midnight. Suddenly, as I stood by the medlar tree, which faces Milton's mulberry, I started at hearing the door by Christ's Pieces shut with a distinct noise. Standing still I listened, and heard the sound which I had heard once before of a body brushing through the shrubs. My mind was full of Collier, and I had little doubt that this was he. Peering through the bushes I saw a figure moving slowly along.

I stepped to a spot near by where the removal of some dead shrubs had given a clear view of the bathing pool. As I did so the figure which I knew to be that of Collier stumbled through the bushes on the further side of the pool and stood on the grass path that borders it. He was within a foot or two of the water. For a moment he stood still, as though hesitating and uncertain of his whereabouts; he passed his hands over his face, and I noticed that he had no hat. The gesture gave the impression of someone half dazed trying in vain to sweep away the mists that clouded his brain. Then he began to move up the path towards the garden house. He swayed heavily and brushed into the bushes; righting himself he advanced till he was a quarter of a length from the end of the path. Then he stumbled again, and all but fell into the water. This appeared to frighten him, for he turned suddenly in the path and walked the other way, traversing half the length of the bath in that direction. He was now beside the deeper water, where it is quite six feet to the bottom of the bath. Suddenly he gave a fearful lurch towards the bushes, made a violent effort to recover himself, and in so doing put one foot right on the edge of the path. The soft soil gave way under the pressure. I saw him throw out his arms as if to recover his balance, but the attempt failed, and with a suppressed cry he fell headlong into the water.

Now Collier, as I knew, was a good and powerful swimmer; we had often bathed together in the swimming bath. But he seemed dazed and struggled feebly in the water. I had been in great doubt as to what to do. To have shouted to him when on the path would have startled him, and perhaps have precipitated the catastrophe. There was no time to reach him and guide him from his dangerous path; to do that it would have been necessary to walk to the bath and half-way round it. But on seeing him fall I plunged through the bushes and emerged beside the water, near the urn which commemorates Joseph Mede.[1] Collier was struggling in the deep end near the middle line of the bath, and was about six feet from the bank, where are the busts of Milton and Cudworth.[2]

Lying on the bank I could see the long pole with a heavy iron hook at the end, which is used for reaching things in the water and for raising the gate of the sluice. Picking it up I turned it towards Collier, when I noticed that his struggles were propelling him towards the bank where I stood. At that moment a feeling of nausea and rage overwhelmed me. What I had intended to do with the pole I do not know clearly, but as I became aware that Collier might reach the bank and escape a red mist seemed to envelop me in the darkness. After all, his infernal luck was going to hold good again. I determined that it should not. I believe I had gone to him with the intention of helping him, but the sight of his getting out of his scrape on his own account turned any kindly intentions I might have had to wrath. Was the man endowed with supernatural good fortune? Any other would have drowned like a dog as he deserved! Creeping in in a state of

---

[1] This memorial urn may still be seen. It stands half-way down the bath on the left-hand side on leaving the garden-house. Joseph Mede was a distinguished Fellow and Dean of Christ's, 1603-38. He died in the latter year at the age of 52. In 1627 he refused the offer of the Provostship of Trinity College, Dublin. He was a master of many subjects and noted for his candour and liberality. He lived in the present reading room and is buried in the Chapel "in the middle of the area on the south side."

[2] These still stand on the same bank, at the end of the bath furthest from the house.

beastliness and intoxication! The thought of Mary Clifford came to my mind. So kind, good and dignified! To be allied with this drunkard struggling in the water! Surely anything was better than to allow that!

A gleam of moonlight through the trees struck on Collier's upturned face, and his eyes fixed themselves on mine as I stood with the pole outstretched. At that instant I let the pole drop. The heavy hooked end struck him on the left temple. His head fell back and he disappeared.

That was the last I saw, and practically the last that I heard of Philip Collier.

THE RECORD OF CHRISTOPHER ROUND

PART IV. RETROSPECT

(1)

How I regained my rooms I know not. I suppose that the experiences of the night threw me into a fever, for I became seriously ill and unconscious. When I came to myself they told me that I had been ill for weeks, and I had to go away for a year to the South of England. I returned to my work at the College when the year was ended. No one ever spoke to me of Collier, and, as I could hardly bear to think of him, I never referred to him. How his death was explained I never asked. I presume that it was regarded as an accident. No one ever suspected the truth.

(2)

I found on my return after my illness that Mary Clifford had left Cambridge soon after I went away, and I never heard from her again, after Collier died, except for one kind note of enquiry, which came while I was ill. I did not reply to it, since I felt myself unfit to approach her after the thing that I had done. She did not keep up with any of her acquaintances at Cambridge, and I presume that Collier's death made her wish to forget it and most of its associations. She died at Herford House, near Nottingham, the home of her old friends, Mr. and Mrs. George Stanley. That was about ten years after Collier's death.

I saw in the daily journal that the contents of her house in London were to be sold, and, happening to be in town on the day, I purchased a catalogue, and my eye caught an item marked "Lot 60." It consisted of two miniatures in a leathern case. Feeling sure that these must be the ones I had seen years before I decided to purchase them. I have them still, and at times gaze at them as I did on the day when I began this narration. I shall

# #

keep them till I die and then bequeath them to Simon[1] to dispose of as he thinks fit. They are beautifully executed, and Collier must have finished the one of himself. It is masterly. On the back, in Mary's writing, is the word "Philip," and on the back of her own she had written her own name and added "Given to me by Philip." Thus I know that she loved him.

It is twenty years since she died, and each time that I look at her, her gracious presence seems back with me again. In all these years I have seen no human being who so personified gentleness and grace. Perhaps somewhere we may be permitted to meet, and I may gain forgiveness from them both.

(3)

As the years have passed I feel that I have made some expiation for what I did. I have served the College faithfully, but I have refused all advancement both in College and University. I have lived on in these old rooms almost as a recluse, seeing my pupils and a few old friends and scarcely anyone else. I have had no intimates, except Simon Goodridge, and even to him I could never reveal the truth. What life has been with this remembrance always haunting me none but myself will ever know. That has been a retribution in itself.

I take an almost daily walk in the garden as far as the end of the great lawn. For thirty years I have not penetrated to the lower garden.

Occasionally I walk in the country by the old Manor at Chesterton, where I passed the happiest days of my life. I sometimes think I can still see Mary Clifford smiling a greeting from the little room over the porch, as she used to do. May God give her rest!

I have told the truth, and in due course it will be made known. I have written it now because I feel that those who come after should know me as I am. I am called a benefactor of the College because I have given it some things. I shall give it more when I die. I do not desire that in those after times I should be commemorated as a better man than I am.

May God, to whom I commend my spirit, forgive me my sins, especially that which I have here confessed.

CHRISTOPHER ROUND.

---

[1] Simon Goodridge, Fellow and Tutor of Christ's College. For the final disposition of the miniatures *see* Simon Goodridge's recollections appended to this record.

III

(From the papers collected by Simon Goodridge)

[Extract from the *Isle of Ely and Cambridgeshire Gazette*]

THE SAD DEATH OF A FELLOW OF CHRIST'S COLLEGE

INQUEST ON MR. PHILIP COLLIER

The Coroner of the town of Cambridge, Mr. R. P. Snow, attorney-at-law, held an inquest at the Guildhall concerning the death of Mr. Philip Collier, the brilliant classical scholar of Christ's College.

The circumstances of his death will already be familiar to our readers. On Tuesday morning, John Avenel, a milkman, crossing Christ's Pieces in the early hours, discovered the body of a man lying in Milton's Walk, which runs along the Pieces outside the wall of Christ's College Fellows' Garden. Avenel, seeing that the man was unconscious, went for help, and found a watchman, John Bruce, in King Street. Bruce ran for Doctor Greatorex, the physician, who resides at Little Trinity,[1] in Jesus Lane. Dr. Greatorex was not there, but Bruce found him at the house of his son and partner, Mr. Edward Greatorex, in Bridge Street.[2] Dr. Greatorex, on arriving, recognised Mr. Collier, and found, on examination, that life was already extinct. The body was removed to the mortuary.

We append below an account of the proceedings at the inquest.

The Coroner, Mr. R. P. Snow, addressing the jury, said that all would regret the sudden ending of what promised to be, and had been, a brilliant

---

[1] This house still exists. It is a fine Georgian building on the left-hand side of Jesus Lane, approaching it from Sidney Street. It stands back in a garden almost at the corner of Park Street.

[2] This eighteenth-century house still stands almost opposite to the entrance to the Union Society and the Round Church. It is at present occupied by Dr. J. R. C. Canney.

career. Mr. Collier was well known in the University, had a great reputation as a scholar, and was much liked. There were some points that needed to be cleared up before they could be sure as to how he had met his death. He would call the necessary witnesses at once, and the jury, after hearing their evidence, would, he hoped, be able to form a definite opinion.

The first witness was Dr. Caleb Parkins, Bursar of Christ's College, who identified the body as that of Mr. Philip Collier, one of the Fellows and a Classical Lecturer at Christ's College. He saw Mr. Collier on Tuesday afternoon, when he dined in Hall, and last saw him in the court on Wednesday morning. He appeared to be in his usual health, which was generally good.

John Avenel, milkman, deposed to finding the body and fetching the watchman, John Bruce; the latter, giving evidence, said that he immediately went for Dr. Greatorex, and returned and helped him in examining the body.

Doctor Marmaduke Greatorex, physician, was then called. He said he was Doctor of Medicine of the University and a member of Jesus College. In the early hours of Thursday morning he was called by the last witness, John Bruce, and proceeded with him to Christ's Pieces. In Milton's Walk, about one-third of the length of the Walk from the King Street end, he found the body of a man. It was guarded by John Avenel, the milk-man, who had found it, and he said it had not been moved since first discovered. The body lay on its side. He turned it on its back, and recognised Mr. Philip Collier, a well-known Fellow of Christ's College. He soon found that life was extinct. There was no outward sign of injury, except a deep wound on the left temple. It was difficult to say how this wound had been inflicted, but from some of the facts that had come to light he had surmised the following: beside the body was a high iron hurdle lying on its side, and the shape of the wound on the temple seemed to show that it had been inflicted by Mr. Collier falling on one of the iron uprights of the hurdle. One other fact he noticed particularly was that the clothing was very wet. He had the body removed to the mortuary and informed the College authorities. Since then he had, in company with Mr. Prentice, surgeon, made a post-mortem examination of the body. They found considerable injury to the brain from the blow on the left temple, and this they considered to be the cause of death. There was some slight valvular disease of the heart. Not sufficient to have caused death or probably much inconvenience, but sufficient to give rise to unpleasant sensations if the heart were suddenly submitted to severe strain. They found nothing else abnormal, except that the lungs appeared to be in a peculiar condition, and to have recently contained a good deal of liquid. This was specially noticed, because the whole body and the clothing were saturated with water. Mr. Collier must certainly have been immersed in water very shortly before his death. He had no hat and his hair was soaked. It had not rained during the night. There was one other point that he ought to mention. A very peculiar odour hung about the body, and was particularly noticeable in a handkerchief, which was found in one of the pockets. What this odour was he could not say, but it certainly reminded him of some preparations containing alcohol.

The Coroner asked the witness if he meant to infer that Mr. Collier had been drinking.

The Witness replied that there was no evidence of that. The smell was unlike that of any alcoholic drink with which he was acquainted. He was unable to explain the wet condition of the clothing, or how Mr. Collier came to fall on the hurdle, but, in his opinion, death was due to the blow on the temple caused by a heavy fall on the iron rod of the hurdle.

The Coroner : You regard it then as an accidental death?

The Witness : I should certainly say so.

Mr. Prentice, surgeon, was then called, and corroborrated the opinions of Dr. Greatorex.

The Coroner, addressing the jury, said that they had heard the medical evidence, and he was sure that they would like some further enlightenment as to Mr. Collier's habits, and particularly as to his movements during the latter part of Wednesday. He therefore called as the next witness the Master of Christ's College.

The Master said that Mr. Collier had been personally known to him for some years. He was a man of the highest character, and abstemious in his habits. He was sure that there was no ground for suggesting that his fatal accident was in any way due to indulgence in strong drink. He understood that this was not suggested by the medical witnesses, but it might be inferred by persons reading the evidence and not having much knowledge of the matter. He could not explain how Mr. Collier came to be in the position in which he was found. He had ascertained that he left the College early in the afternoon, and did not return to it. He had no knowledge of his movements after he left the College.

The Coroner : Had Mr. Collier exhibited any peculiarities or changes in his habits?

The Master : No, except that he had somewhat withdrawn from society lately and had been known to shut himself in his rooms rather early. It was supposed he was engaged in literary work and desired not to be interrupted.

At this point a letter was handed to the Coroner. After reading it he announced to the jury that a witness was forthcoming, who would be able to clear up the mystery as to Mr. Collier's movements after leaving College on Wednesday afternoon. This witness had come forward voluntarily, but could not attend the Court until the afternoon. He therefore proposed to adjourn until then.

The Court reassembled in the afternoon. Mr. Snow, the Coroner, at once called Dr. Simpson, the witness who had communicated with him in the morning.

The Witness said : My name is James Young Simpson, and I am a Doctor of Medicine of Edinburgh University. But first I must apologise to the Court for not being here earlier; I have been away from Cambridge, and only returned today. I had hoped to have been able to see the Coroner before the enquiry opened, but was prevented by a long-standing engagement in London. The facts as far as I know of them are these.

I am an obstetric physician and surgeon at the Edinburgh Infirmary. As perhaps the Court knows, there has been much attention given lately, in America, to the possibility of devising a means of making patients temporarily unconscious, so that they may be treated surgically without pain. In this enquiry I have been greatly interested, as it appears to me that it would be most beneficial in the kind of cases with which I am associated. A short while ago I had the opportunity of meeting some of the American scientists who are engaged in this enquiry, and during the last year I have discussed the matter with them in Paris.

While I was in France I became acquainted with Mr. Collier, who showed the greatest interest in the subject. He said he knew of one or two people at Cambridge who would be willing to help in research of that kind, and, as I was proposing to spend some months in London, I promised to come to Cambridge from time to time, and that we would make experiments together. Whenever I came here I stayed at a house called Croft Holme,[1] in Chesterton Road, which Mr. Collier and a friend of his, Lady Clifford, who was also

---

[1] This house still stands in a large garden, near the turning to Victoria Bridge, but nearer to Jesus Lock. The entrance is in Croft Holme Lane.

interested in our work, rented furnished. My friends, Mr. George Keith and Mr. Duncan, surgeons, of Edinburgh, generally came with me. Our purpose was to make experiments, on one another, of inhaling various preparations to see if we could produce the state of temporary unconsciousness we desired.

The Coroner : A very risky and, I think I may say, a very improper proceeding.

The Witness : There was certainly a risk. We were anxious to keep our researches private until we had arrived at some conclusions favourable, or the reverse. We all, Mr. Keith, Mr. Duncan, Mr. Collier and I, and one or two others who came occasionally, took turns at being the subject of the experiments. Mr. Collier was most enthusiastic. He would not hear of danger, and was always speaking of the glorious gain it would be to humanity if we succeeded. Whenever we were trying any new step, or new agent, he would always be the first to offer himself as the subject. He did not seem to know what fear was.

The Coroner : And did you succeed?

The Witness : We have not succeeded so far, but many times we have appeared to be on the point of achieving what we aimed at.

The Coroner: What were the materials you used?

The Witness : That I would rather not explain in detail. We have tried many mixtures and compounds, but for a long time we tried sulphuric ether, but we are sure that something more conveniently portable and swifter must be found.

The Coroner : And what were the effects of these experiments?

The Witness : We have all of us been rendered almost unconscious, and quite so for a very short time, but we must, of course, do better than that if the process is to be of any practical use.

The Coroner : And do you connect Mr. Collier's death with these, if I may say so, rash and presumptuous experiments?

The Witness : I am sorry to say that I do. Mr. Collier, as I said, was always willing to be a subject. We had not heard that he had any heart trouble such as the doctors say the post-mortem examination has disclosed. Whether he knew of it I cannot say. He was physically a very strong man, and a very brave one. But he told me not so long ago that he should have to be more careful, as he found the experiments left after effects which were disturbing. Sometimes on his way home he had been attacked by giddiness and faintness almost amounting to unconsciousness. So much so that he feared meeting anyone in case he should be over-taken by the symptoms. He told me he always went straight back to his rooms, and had found a way of getting to them without going through the College.

The Coroner : What did you do?

The Witness : I advised him to give up the experiments for a while, which he did. However, his interest continued unabated, and lately he had resumed, and for some reason appeared keener and more impatient than ever to gain a solution of the problem. All the rest of us noticed this particularly. We had a meeting on Wednesday.

The Coroner : What happened then?

The Witness : Mr. Collier arrived in excellent spirits, and Mr. Keith and Mr. Duncan were there too. We were going to test a new mixture which I had devised in London. I need not go into details, but we had thought that by increasing the percentage of alcohol we might attain to the result we desired. Mr. Collier insisted upon being one of the subjects. I spoke to him about the risk of his being ill afterwards; he had to walk home and we had not; but he was quite cheery and confident about it, and declared his belief that we should produce real anæsthesia and solve the problem this time. In the end Mr. Duncan and I administered the drug to Mr. Collier and Mr. Keith.

The Coroner : How did you do that?

The Witness : We had the mixture already concocted, and have an appliance by which the fumes can be inhaled.

The Coroner : What was the result?

The Witness : Almost what we had hoped for. Both subjects became quite unconscious, but again we found they began to recover too quickly for the anæsthesia to be of any practical use. We attempted to give them more of the gas, but the result was that both were sick, so we had to give it up.

The Coroner : It seems a very undesirable proceeding, most reprehensible. What happened to Mr. Collier?

The Witness : He soon pulled round and said he believed the thing could be done if he gave the anæsthetic to himself. He said he could not inhale properly with someone else moving about him. He saturated his own handkerchief and practised inhaling, and then had another serious attempt to make himself unconscious.

The Coroner : Did he succeed?

[Extract from the *Isle of Ely and Cambridgeshire Gazette*.]

MILTON'S WALK, CHRIST'S PIECES.

"I searched Christ's Pieces to see if I could find it, and discovered it in a clump
of bushes, which he passed through on entering the Piece from Belmont Place
and Pike's Walk. It is not far from the ' Horse and Groom ' inn. I picked up the
hat and walked carefully from where it lay towards the garden wall. While
I was looking about, I saw something glistening not far from the wall, and when
I picked it up I found it was a fairly large key."

The Witness : For some reason or other he was less successful than before, and complained that it made him feel very shaky. However, after a while he said he felt better and would walk home, as the air would do him good. We offered to go with him, but he declined rather abruptly and seemed quite cheerful and competent, so we desisted and he left.

The Coroner : At what time was that?

The Witness : It must have been past ten. He had arrived at our house at about six, and said he had been for a long walk over the Gogs and Cherry-hinton and had called to see Lady Clifford, who was a friend of his, at Chesterton Manor before coming to us.

The Coroner : And that was the last that you saw of him?

The Witness : Yes. On Thursday morning I was coming across Midsummer Common when I met Dr. Greatorex, who told me of the accident. I hurried to the spot, and the doctor showed me where the body had lain and also showed me the hurdle.

The Coroner : And what conclusions did you come to?

The Witness : At first I could not make it out. But, when I heard that Mr. Collier was soaked through, I jumped to the conclusion that he had been overtaken by the giddiness of which he had formerly complained and had fallen into the river, which he would have had to cross, probably somewhere opposite to Jesus Close, on his way home. Mr. Collier knew the boat-keepers well, and was in the habit of rowing himself across in any boat he found moored by the yard. I heard too that he was without his hat, which he was certainly wearing when he left our house. I searched Christ's Pieces to see if I could find it, and discovered it in a clump of bushes, which he passed through on entering the Piece from Belmont Place and Pike's Walk. It is not far from the "Horse and Groom" inn.[1] I picked up the hat and walked carefully from where it lay towards the garden wall. While I was looking about, I saw something glistening not far from the wall, and when I picked it up I found it was a fairly large key. The grass about here, and at the spot where I had found the hat, was much depressed, and it seemed to me clear that Mr. Collier had fallen more than once, and had lost his hat the first time and dropped his key afterwards, and had not recovered either in the darkness. I think this explains what happened later.

---

[1] This inn still exists, and may be seen facing Christ's Pieces in the centre of the row of houses on its north side.

The Coroner : How so?

The Witness : I have ascertained that the key is one that fits all the doors and gates leading to and from the Fellows' Garden. It seems obvious that Mr. Collier, who had told us that when he felt giddy after these experiments he used an unobserved way of regaining his rooms, had intended to enter College by the garden door at the end of Christ's Pieces, rather than, in his then condition, which might have been misunderstood, passing through the main gate and the courts. He had already the key in his hand when he stumbled and fell. He was probably dazed and could not find it again. Being unable to open the door, and being unwilling to go to the front gate, he decided to scale the wall with the help of the iron hurdle he found there. He was a very strong man and could easily have managed it in his ordinary condition. But I think that in his dazed state it proved too much for him. He must have mounted the hurdle after propping it against the wall, and it probably slipped while he was on it, and he fell and struck his temple heavily against one of the uprights. His condition was probably worse owing to his immersion in the river.

The Coroner : I am inclined to agree with your views, sir. I do not think we need trouble you further. Much as I regret the very rash experiments in which you have indulged, I am obliged to you for coming forward frankly to enlighten us as to the events that led up to Mr. Collier's death.

The Witness : I can only say in addition how very seriously my colleagues and I regret this dreadful occurrence. Mr. Collier was a dear friend, and we admired his enthusiasm sincerely. It will be a lasting sorrow to us that our researches should have been in any way the cause of his losing his life. We regard him as one of the martyrs in the cause of scientific progress.

The Coroner then proceeded to sum up.

He pointed out that there was no suggestion, or likelihood, of foul play, and suggested that the jury would probably find that the theory put forward by Dr. Simpson was the correct one, and would return a verdict in accordance with the medical evidence. There was no need for him to dwell on the terrible tragedy, which had robbed the University and Christ's College of one of its most promising sons. He did not think he would be committing an indiscretion if he revealed the fact that in Mr. Collier's pocket had been found a letter, still legible, in spite of the soaking it had received, offering him the vacant chair of the Professorship of Greek in the University, lately held by Professor Philpotts. The letter had only reached him on the day he died. It made his loss all the more lamentable.

Before concluding, he felt it his duty to address a few remarks to Dr. Simpson and the other young men associated with him in the experiments he had described. They now saw the dangers to which such things led. But, apart from that, there was another aspect of the case. No doubt scientific knowledge was a great and useful thing, and its advancement was to be encouraged. There were even some who prophesied that in times to come their University would give much time and thought to the patronage of the Natural Sciences. That might be so. These things might prove to be useful adjuncts to the studies of the humanities and other branches of the higher learning. But there were limits to what it was lawful, or expedient, to do; there were some things in which it was a presumption to meddle. It seemed to him that these young men, well meaning no doubt, had presumed to pass that limit. From of old it had been decreed by Providence that pain was part of the life and punishment of man and of woman. All regretted it, but all must bear their part of the common burden, which was the consequence of our earliest forefathers' sin. This attempt to defeat the ordinances of the Almighty and the laws of Nature by artificial means, savoured of the impious, and could but end in disaster. Man was born in pain, and this attempt of Dr. Simpson, which, from his special practice, he understood to be chiefly aimed at destroying the pangs of birth, for which they had Biblical authority, should be discountenanced by all right-thinking men. He felt sure that even if his experiments should be successful few religious women would avail themselves of such aids. Both morally and physically the danger from their use was very great. It was not his place formally to censure Dr. Simpson and his friends, but he had felt it his duty to make these remarks, and he hoped that the shock they had received would be a lesson to them to desist from these practices in future.

For Mr. Collier, whose rashness they greatly lamented, they felt much sorrow. They understood that he had few near relatives, but he was sure that all would feel sympathy with those to whom he was near and dear in their grief, and with the Master and Fellows of Christ's College in the loss of one of their most brilliant colleagues.

The Master and Fellows, he might add, were in much trouble just now, as the Master had informed him that another of their body, the Reverend Christopher Round, was seriously ill, having had some sort of seizure on the night Mr. Collier met with his death.

The jury, after a short deliberation, returned a verdict of "Accidental death by a blow on the head caused by a fall, resulting in the injuries as described in the medical evidence."

They desired to associate themselves heartily with the remarks made by the Coroner on the reprehensible practices indulged in by Dr. Simpson, Mr. Collier, and their friends.

IV

(*From the papers collected by Simon Goodridge*)

[Extract from the *East Anglian Times*]

WILL OF THE LATE MR. PHILIP COLLIER OF CHRIST'S COLLEGE

The will has just been published of the late Mr. Philip Collier, who died under tragic circumstances, as our readers will remember. By it he appointed Dr. Caleb Parkins, Bursar of Christ's College, his executor, and bequeathed to him fifty guineas. He left his books to Christ's College Library, subject to the condition that his friend, Mary Clifford, widow of Sir Henry Clifford, should have the right of choosing twenty volumes for herself. Having no near relations by blood, the will goes on to state, the testator left all the rest of his property (with the exception of five hundred pounds, which he bequeathed to the Master and Fellows of Christ's College for the general good of that Foundation, and fifty pounds to the same body for the purchase of plate in memory of him) to the said Mary Clifford.

He left particular instructions to his executor to see that a case, containing two miniatures painted by himself, should, with its contents, be given to Lady Clifford at once, if it was not already in her possession when he died.

It is interesting to note, considering the circumstances of Mr. Collier's death, that he recognised the risk he was running. The will was made only a week or two before he died, and is witnessed by his College servant and the latter's wife. In it Mr. Collier states that he was making it because he intended to embark on a fresh series of experiments very soon, when Dr. Simpson returned to Cambridge, and, in view of the results of previous experiences and the effects he had suffered, he had decided to put his affairs in order in case of mishap.

It is hard to say whether the courage of the testator should be admired more than his temerity should be censured, or the reverse.

The value of the estate was sworn at two thousand and two hundred pounds.

V

THE RECOLLECTIONS OF SIMON GOODRIDGE

(*From the papers collected, by Simon Goodridge*)

The paper written by Christopher Round was left to me at his death. He had spoken to me of it, but had never discussed its contents, of which I was ignorant. I understood that he wished me to read it, but not to communicate it to others, and it was not to be published for fifty years after his death. I shall not live so long as that, and I have decided to put the papers in order and add to them such comments as I can and then to leave them in trustworthy hands when I go.

I have placed with Round's paper two newspaper extracts, one giving the account of the inquest on Philip Collier and the other an account of his will.

In this paper I am putting down what I can recollect of the happenings at the time of Collier's death and Round's illness. I was in residence as a new Junior Fellow at the time.

Round died two or three years after writing his narrative. In his later years he became more friendly with me than with anyone else here, so that I am anxious for his sake to say what I know. I only knew Collier slightly. In what little intercourse I had with him he attracted me greatly.

As far as I am able to say the statements Round makes about his general career are correct and trustworthy. I recollect the great interest that was taken in his competition with Collier for the Chair of Greek when Dr. Philpotts resigned. Most of us thought that Round would be appointed as he was a sounder, if less brilliant, scholar than Collier. But I remember how opinion gradually went round in favour of Collier, chiefly on account of the dulness of Round's lectures, which, it was generally noticed, fell off very much in quality about that time. No one knew how to account for Round's failure, but he seemed out of health. He would take long walks in the country, and spent much time strolling about the garden by himself. He seemed to get more reserved and morose. Collier, on the other hand, was particularly lively, though we did not see very much of him. He was popularly supposed to spend his evenings by himself for the purpose of writing a book on his Italian studies, and it was freely hinted by the gossips that he was, or soon would be, engaged to Lady Clifford, whom I only knew slightly.

My recollections of the day when Philip Collier met with his death are somewhat vague, but I remember one or two incidents clearly. During the morning I had occasion to call upon Round, and found him very gloomy and apparently ill. He said that he was not very well, and I recommended him to go to bed early that night. Late in the evening I happened to meet Mason, Round's gyp, and asked him how Mr. Round was. He replied that he had not been at all well in the afternoon, and had been lying down, but had remarked that he would take a turn in the garden, as was often his custom, before going to bed. I went up to see how he was getting on about nine o'clock in the evening, but, though I could see that a lamp was burning in his rooms, the door was closed. An hour or so later I passed through the court and observed that the lamp was out in his sitting-room, so I concluded he had gone to bed.

So far as I know no one actually saw Round, after his gyp left him, until next morning. Mason arrived about six o'clock, and on going to Round's rooms was horrified to find Round lying at full length on the floor. He noticed that the lamp was burning in the sitting-room. Round was dressed as he usually was when walking in the garden. Beside him was a heavy stick.

Mason got him back to bed, and after that called me. We sent for the doctor. Round was seriously ill, and wandered in his mind, muttering incoherently. The Doctor said it was some kind of seizure, and probably the result of overwork. Round remained unconscious for a long time.

Some weeks after, when he was partially recovered, someone mentioned Collier's death in his presence. The effect was alarming; we had forgotten that he could not have heard of it, as he was taken ill the night it happened. It threw him into a paroxysm of agitation, which brought on a serious relapse. I do not think that anyone ever ventured to refer to Collier in his presence again.

Eventually he recovered sufficiently to go away to the seaside, and he was absent from Cambridge, as he says, for a year. When he came back he seemed quite well again, but we all noticed a change in him. He saw his pupils and lectured, and was most punctual and attentive to business. He was kindness itself to his pupils, always patient and sincere, and a warm and generous supporter of charities and college institutions. But he was more reserved than ever. That his illness had left permanent effects we gathered from certain peculiarities which he exhibited and from the fact that he would accept no kind of promotion, and remained for the rest of his life merely a College Lecturer. He could have had Univeristy posts, and almost any position he liked in College. We supposed that his illness had weakened him so much that he dreaded responsibility. He never referred to Collier, and by tacit consent the latter was never mentioned when he was present, nor was any remark made about the Professorship of Greek. We all supposed that he must have heard the tragedy of Collier's death spoken of while he was believed to be unconscious and in his weakened state it had left a permanent impression on his mind. Hence his dread of the subject.

Among the peculiarities which we noticed in him was this. Though he used the garden more than any of the other Fellows, he never went beyond the upper garden. The great yew tree and the ash tree formed the boundary marks of his walk, and nothing could induce him to go beyond there. To such an extent did he carry this idiosyncracy that he would not eat the mulberries from Milton's tree when they were served in Hall, or in the Combination Room. At the time this was merely regarded as a prejudice, which his illness had given him against this kind of fruit, but in the light of what he has written I am inclined to assign to it another cause.

When Round died he left me a leathern box containing the miniatures of Philip Collier and Mary Clifford to dispose of as I thought fit. They appeared to me to be very fine pieces of work, and, finding that this opinion was held by experts whom I consulted, I offered them to the Fitzwilliam Museum, by whom they were accepted.

Now as to Philip Collier and his researches.

There seems no doubt that he was greatly attracted by novelty, or discovery, of any kind, but he had not shown any great interest in medicine or science. It seemed, therefore, that there must have been other reasons to account for his extreme interest in Dr. Simpson's researches and, especially, for his taking up the experiments again after repeated warnings of the dangerous effects some of them had had on him. Whether he knew that there was anything definitely the matter with his heart I do not know, but I think not. These other reasons I think I can explain.

Lady Clifford died, as Round relates, about ten years after Collier. A few years later, about five I think, Mr. (afterwards Sir Isaac) Playfair, then one of the leading physicians at Nottingham, dined with us in Hall. I had a long conversation with him in the Combination Room, and finding that we had tastes in common I asked him up to my rooms. While there he happened to say he had been to see a friend who lived at Chesterton Manor, and he asked if I knew it. This led me to mention Lady Clifford, in whose time I had been there once, and Dr. Playfair became very interested. It appeared that he had attended Lady Clifford in her last illness, and he told me that, had the discoveries in anæsthetics which had since been made been known then, it would have been possible to have attempted to save her life. She had apparently suffered from an internal complaint of long standing. She told Dr. Playfair that she had been aware of it for some years, and she had hoped at one time that the advance in the knowledge of anæsthetics would be made sufficiently rapidly for it to be of use to her, as a surgical operation was the only chance of cure. But, she added, she had found that it was dangerous to experiment with these drugs, and had of late years avoided interest in the subject and determined to bear her troubles as best she could.

Dr. Playfair said it was a sad thing that nothing could then be done, as she was still comparatively young, not more than forty-five, I believe, and in full vigour of mind.

This conversation interested me, for I think it explains the sustained enthusiasm of Philip Collier for a subject far removed from his own studies. He had heard of Dr. Simpson's endeavours to find a reliable anæsthetic, and had heartily co-operated with him out of love of adventure and to advance knowledge. When he experienced such serious effects he temporarily desisted as Dr. Simpson said. But later he had become acquainted, I think, with the fact that Mary Clifford suffered from a complaint which could only be cured by a surgical operation, for which a condition of anæsthesia was necessary. Finding that Dr. Simpson was about to try some new experiments, he insisted on taking part in them in spite of the warnings he had formerly received, in the hope of benefiting the woman he loved. The results we know. That he was aware of the danger he was facing is shown by his remarks in making his will, and by his making the will at that time. It makes his career all the more striking and deepens the tragedy.

Many Christ's men have given their lives in the past for the sake of friends, or for the advancement of knowledge, and many, without doubt, will do so in the future. But to few has it been given to do both so directly.

Philip Collier, throwing away his great chances in life and sacrificing it all for the woman he greatly and worthily loved and for the advancement of knowledge in its most beneficent form, is a figure of inspiration, worthy of respect, and entitled to enrolment amongst the greatest of the College heroes. In all our history we have produced few men more attractive, more courageous, or more scholarly than Philip Collier.

His death was a great blow to Dr. Simpson and his colleagues, and they gave up their researches for some while, so that it was not until years later that the solution of the problem was at last found by them at Edinburgh,[1] which place, therefore, has the credit of this great discovery, a credit which, but for the tragedy of Collier's death, might have attached to Cambridge.

On Christopher Round's account of how Philip Collier met his death I purposely refrain from comment. It must be left to any who may chance to read this record to judge for themselves. There is Round's statement, there is the account at the inquest. One of them may be true and the other not; there may be truth in both. I have merely tried to add details which may assist arrival at the truth. Is it possible that to a mind constantly dwelling on one subject the physical presence of the person concerned may set going a train of thought which, though merely suggestive, may seem to the thinker afterwards to be fact? For Collier must have been approaching the garden wall while Round was dwelling on him and on his troubles. Or was the inquest evidence wrong, and did Round do what he says he did, and did Collier somehow get out of the water and the garden?

Each who reads this must judge for himself. But in judging, let him remember how easy it is in this life to be mistaken; easy to be mistaken as to facts, and far easier as to motives, which are always mixed. Round was mistaken in his judgment of Collier, though the evidence appeared to him so conclusive. For one of the lessons of life seems to be to think twice, at least, before judging, and more than thrice before condemning.

For myself I do not desire to occupy the judgment seat, and I am not a psychologist.

SIMON GOODRIDGE.

---

[1] The problem of producing sufficiently prolonged anæsthesia with reasonable safety was solved by Dr. J. Y. Simpson, assisted by the two friends mentioned as taking part in the experiments with Philip Collier, namely, Mr. George Keith and Mr. Duncan.

VI

EDITOR'S POSTSCRIPT

While preparing these papers for the press the following additional evidence bearing on the apparition has come to my notice. My friend, Captain S. R., was, last year, in residence in the Fellows' Building, engaged in training the Cadets quartered at Christ's. He occupied the rooms once inhabited by Philip Collier. Subsequently he went again to the front. Returning on leave this summer he mentioned to me one evening in my rooms that a curious thing happened when he was in residence here last year. He was looking from his window on the garden late one evening in May when he saw the figure of a tall, heavy, elderly man emerge from the chestnuts on the left of the garden and walk slowly down the lawn. From his window he cannot see far down the right side of the garden, but as far as he could tell in the moonlight the man stopped at the lower end of the lawn. Though he waited for a long time to see him reappear and leave the garden, he saw him no more. The man's dress was not quite like that of any one here now, neither did Captain R. recognise him. Being ordered abroad almost directly afterwards, he had no opportunity of mentioning the matter before. I asked him if he could tell me the exact date, and he said he could, because it happened to be on his own birthday, May 29th.

At the end of the Long Vacation this year, another friend, H. C., invalided after service in France, who has occupied rooms for some time in the Fellows' Building, was dining with me in Hall. He was living in the rooms one door above those that belonged to Round. He said that one evening in the May Term he saw an elderly, old-fashioned man walking in the garden in the moonlight, and asked who he was. I asked what the man did, and H. C. said that he came out from under the chestnuts and walked as far as the great yew, where he halted with a kind of jerk, made a right turn, and came up the garden under the green and copper beech trees. Then he disappeared, and, curiously, never came into sight again, though he watched for him for some time. He was, he said, a tall, heavy man dressed in black, with a large, apparently, beaver hat, and what looked like a high stock, his hands were folded behind him, and he carried in them a heavy stick. His head was much bent. The moonlight was very bright, and it was about eleven-thirty. H. C. said it was a curious evening altogether. For, some time after, having given up hopes of seeing the figure again, he was reading at the table in the centre of his room, when he heard a very heavy step slowly ascending the stairs. It came as far as the first door, and stopped at the Senior Tutor's rooms (Round's). He heard the doors open and shut. Knowing that the Senior Tutor was away, he supposed that he had either returned unexpectedly or that he had lent his rooms to a guest. The bedmaker happened to mention in the morning that the Tutor was still away, and H. C. asked her if anyone had occupied the rooms on the previous evening, and she said no. He remembered that this occurred the morning after he had seen the man in the garden, but he did not connect the incident of the figure in the garden with the incident of the footsteps on the stairs. I asked him if he could tell me the exact date. He said he could not, but he could find out, because he went to London on the following day and signed some papers there which he had in his rooms. He afterwards told me that the night of these events was May 29th.

In consequence of the communications of S. R. and H. C. I enquired into the day of the month on which Philip Collier died. I find that his Fellowship ended through his death on May 29th.

Did Round really do what he says he did on May 29th? Does the fact that he still haunts the garden strengthen the belief that his record is true? Or is it that, in the regions of spirit, intention, or even desire, brings the same responsibility as accomplished fact?

A. P. B.

Ingram Content Group UK Ltd.
Milton Keynes UK
UKHW021325300623
424359UK00007B/20